My Gnome on the Roam

on the Roam

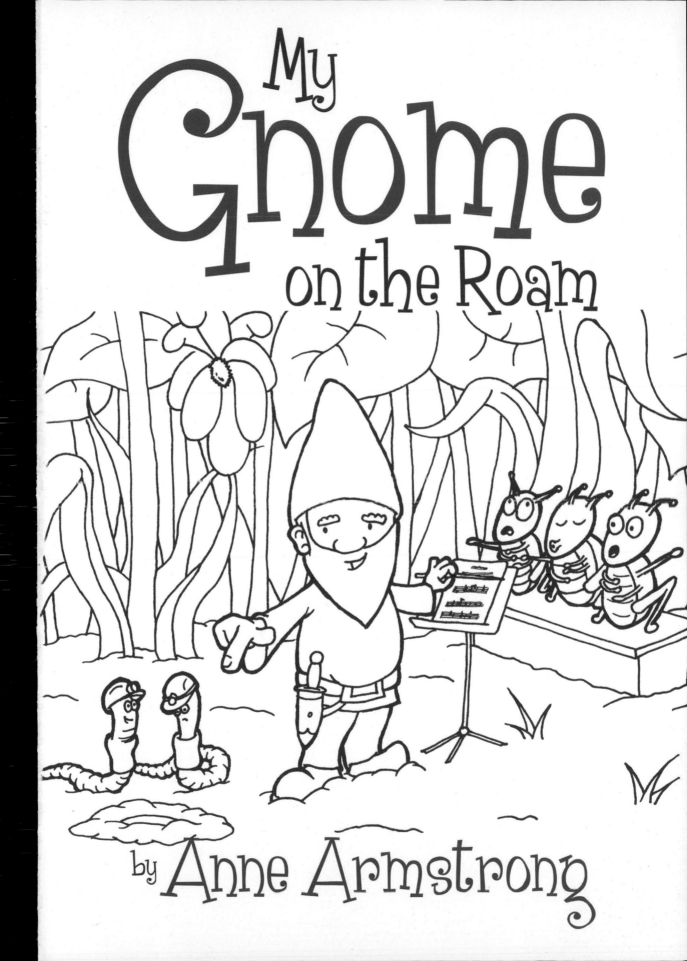

by Anne Armstrong

My Gnome on the Roam
All Rights Reserved.
Copyright © 2015 Anne Armstrong
v2.0 r1.0

Cover Image by Anne Armstrong

Outskirts Press, Inc.
http://www.outskirtspress.com

ISBN: 978-1-4787-4014-8

Library of Congress Control Number: 2014915436

Outskirts Press and the "OP" logo are trademarks belonging to Outskirts, Press, Inc.

PRINTED IN CHINA

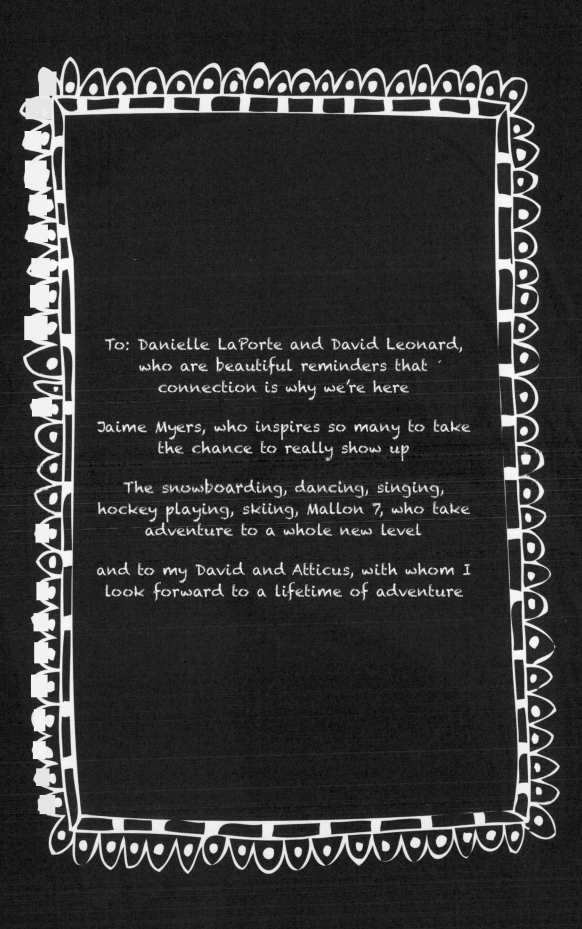

To: Danielle LaPorte and David Leonard,
who are beautiful reminders that
connection is why we're here

Jaime Myers, who inspires so many to take
the chance to really show up

The snowboarding, dancing, singing,
hockey playing, skiing, Mallon 7, who take
adventure to a whole new level

and to my David and Atticus, with whom I
look forward to a lifetime of adventure

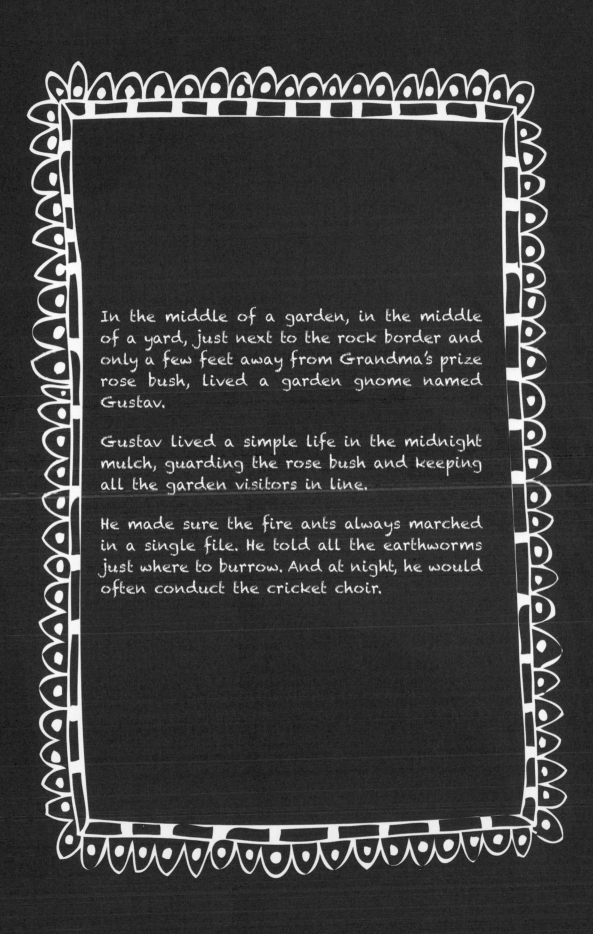

In the middle of a garden, in the middle of a yard, just next to the rock border and only a few feet away from Grandma's prize rose bush, lived a garden gnome named Gustav.

Gustav lived a simple life in the midnight mulch, guarding the rose bush and keeping all the garden visitors in line.

He made sure the fire ants always marched in a single file. He told all the earthworms just where to burrow. And at night, he would often conduct the cricket choir.

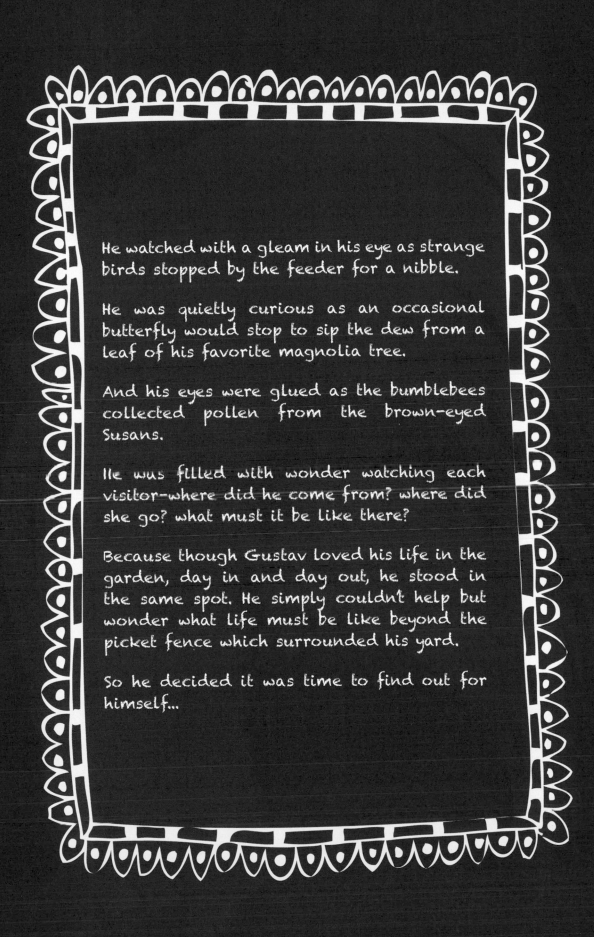

He watched with a gleam in his eye as strange birds stopped by the feeder for a nibble.

He was quietly curious as an occasional butterfly would stop to sip the dew from a leaf of his favorite magnolia tree.

And his eyes were glued as the bumblebees collected pollen from the brown-eyed Susans.

He was filled with wonder watching each visitor-where did he come from? where did she go? what must it be like there?

Because though Gustav loved his life in the garden, day in and day out, he stood in the same spot. He simply couldn't help but wonder what life must be like beyond the picket fence which surrounded his yard.

So he decided it was time to find out for himself...

He boldly asked the next sparrow that landed on the feeder, "What is the world like beyond my picket fence?" The sparrow chirped of great forests with trees as big as skyscrapers. (Of course, Gustav had no idea what a skyscraper was, but still he nodded politely.)

Then he asked the butterfly as she basked in the sun on the magnolia leaf, "What is the world like beyond my picket fence?" The butterfly whispered of a lovely-sounding place called Mexico, where all her Monarch friends agreed to meet each year for a giant butterfly party. (Of course, Gustav had no idea what a Mexico was, but still he nodded politely.)

He cautiously asked the bee hovering over the brown-eyed Susans, "What is the world like beyond my picket fence?" The bee buzzed about fragrant botanical gardens filled with flowers of every color and shape. (Of course, Gustav had no idea what a botanical was, but still he nodded politely.)

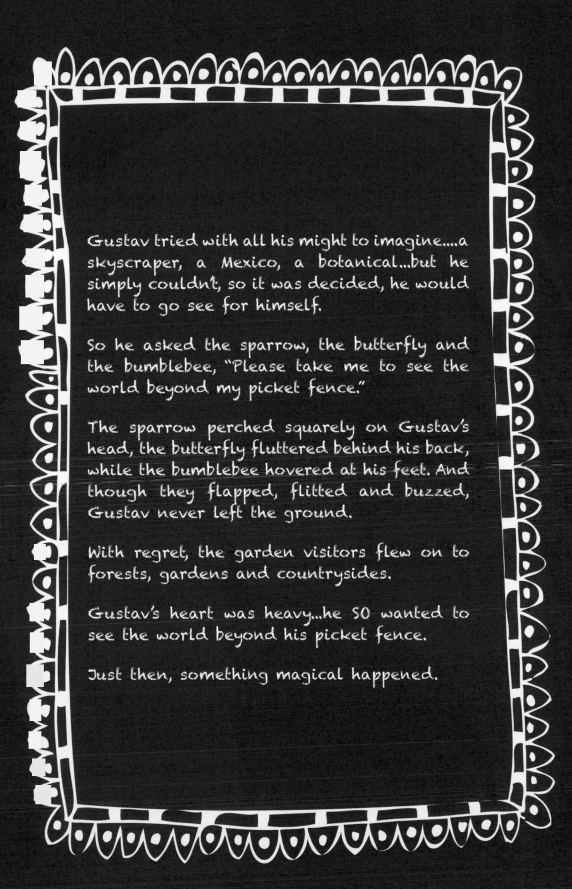

Gustav tried with all his might to imagine....a skyscraper, a Mexico, a botanical...but he simply couldn't, so it was decided, he would have to go see for himself.

So he asked the sparrow, the butterfly and the bumblebee, "Please take me to see the world beyond my picket fence."

The sparrow perched squarely on Gustav's head, the butterfly fluttered behind his back, while the bumblebee hovered at his feet. And though they flapped, flitted and buzzed, Gustav never left the ground.

With regret, the garden visitors flew on to forests, gardens and countrysides.

Gustav's heart was heavy...he SO wanted to see the world beyond his picket fence.

Just then, something magical happened.

The garden gate flew open, and down the path skipped a little girl. She darted past Gustav and leapt into the outstretched arms of her grandmother, who was waiting on the porch.

Later that afternoon, the little girl skipped around the yard, picking flowers, and watching the garden visitors. Just as the sun began to set and grandma called for the little girl to come in, she stopped just next to the garden patch, scooped Gustav into her arms and carried him inside.

Once inside, she set Gustav on a small, round table, covered by a lace doily. He was delighted!

His eyes darted around the room to the peaceful watercolor paintings hanging on the walls. His ears perked as the cuckoo clock clucked out a rhythm. His mouth began to water as he smelled chocolate chip cookies wafting from the kitchen.

Bright and early the next morning, the little girl carried Gustav out the front door and plunked him into a flowered basket which hung from the handlebars of her bicycle. Together, they pedaled and glided through the front gate and down the sidewalk.

He was wide-eyed as he coasted past each house, garden and the other picket fences. He grinned proudly as he was spied by the other garden gnomes.

That afternoon, the little girl tucked Gustav into a picnic basket and took him along as she and grandma enjoyed lunch at the park. He lay on the soft blanket, staring as the breeze blew through a willow tree, children giggled on the swing set, and a number of ducks sailed on the tiny pond.

Just as they were preparing to pack up the basket and head home, grandma pulled a small camera from her purse. She asked a kind stranger to take a picture as she stood in front of the pond with the little girl, who scooped up Gustav without a second thought.

Each day, the little girl, her grandma and Gustav enjoyed a little adventure. They soaked in the sights, sounds, smells and tastes of the world beyond his picket fence.

And with each new adventure, was a new photograph of the three as they visited each site.

In the evenings, Gustav would watch from the table as grandma and the little girl added each photograph to a scrapbook and wrote a little story of the adventure they had taken.

Sadly, the day came when the little girl was to return home to her family. Just as she was about to zip her suitcase, a smile crept across her grandma's face. With a twinkle in her eye, grandma handed Gustav to her.

"Take him home with you. Let him share your adventures. Take plenty of pictures and send them to me. That way, it will be almost like I am sharing the adventures with you."

The little girl was delighted and promised to send pictures of each new place she visited and adventure she embarked upon.

Together, Gustav and the little girl traveled far and wide.

They built sandcastles at the ocean. They fished for trout in a mountain stream. They spelunked in deep caves.

When summer was over, the little girl went back to school and Gustav was placed on a shelf in the living room. Day after day, he awaited a new adventure. But the little girl's hours were filled with homework and dance class, play dates and Girl Scouts. He began to fear that he would never again enjoy the sights, sounds, smells and tastes from beyond his picket fence. He missed the familiar whirrs of the cricket choir. He tried to conduct the cuckoo clock on the wall, but it completely ignored him. He gathered the dust (which was collecting on the shelf around him) and tried to build a sandcastle, but it simply wouldn't hold its shape, no matter how hard Gustav tried.

One rainy Saturday, the little girl invited a friend over to play. As she arrived, she immediately spotted Gustav sitting on the shelf. She asked the little girl his name. The little girl excitedly told her friend all about Gustav and their summer adventures.

Her friend's eyes widened. She told the little girl about her own family's plans to visit the Grand Canyon. She wondered if she might bring Gustav along to share the adventure. The little girl happily agreed on the condition that her friend take a picture with Gustav so that she could share the adventure with her friend.

From that day on, whenever the little girl's family or friends traveled near or far, Gustav was invited to travel along. And with each picture, the little girl learned more about the world. She also learned more about her family and friends by sharing their adventures through stories and pictures.

She began to fill page after page with different adventures—tastes, smells, sounds, history...and created more and more beautiful memories.

Now it's time to begin creating your own
memories, taking your own adventures, and
telling your own stories. Where will you and
your gnome go? What will you do? What is
the world like beyond your picket fence?

Your adventure is just beginning.

Visit us at
www.mygnomeontheroam.com
to join the Adventurer's Club for inspiration,
ideas, to download our app of 15-minute
family adventures and to purchase
your very own Gnome and Adventure Kit.

Gustav by Camilla Spadafino